A St

The Japanese Americans: Prisoners at Home

by
Godwin Chu

Don Johnston Incorporated
Volo, Illinois

Edited by:
Jerry Stemach, MS, CCC-SLP
AAC Specialist, Adaptive Technology Center, Sonoma County, California

Gail Portnuff Venable, MS, CCC-SLP
Speech-Language Pathologist, Scottish Rite Center for Childhood Language Disorders, San Francisco, California

Dorothy Tyack, MA
Learning Disabilities Specialist, Scottish Rite Center for Childhood Language Disorders, San Francisco, California

Consultant: Ted S. Hasselbring, PhD
Professor of Special Education, Vanderbilt University, Nashville, TN

Cover Design: Susan Baptist and Karyl Shields
Cover Photographs: The Bancroft Library, University of California, Berkeley and Corbis Images
Interior Illustrations: Jeff Ham
Read by: Joe Sikora
Sound Engineer: Tom Krol, *TK Audio Studios*
Acknowledgements: Susan Snyder, *The Bancroft Library, University of California, Berkeley*

Published by:

Don Johnston Incorporated
26799 West Commerce Drive
Volo, IL 60073
800.999.4660 USA Canada
800.889.5242 Tech Support
www.donjohnston.com

International Standard Book Number
ISBN 1-58702-364-4

Contents

For Miyoko and Takeo Yuki

Your family has blessed America.

Chapter 1

The Attack on Pearl Harbor

In 1941, Johnny Ohashi lived in San Francisco, California, with his mother, father and grandmother. In those days, there was no TV, so they all sat around the radio every night after dinner. They listened to music by big bands. They also listened to other programs on the radio. One of Johnny's favorite programs was a mystery called "The Shadow." Another one of his favorite programs was an adventure called "The Lone Ranger."

At 9 o'clock, Johnny's family listened to the news. There was always news about World War II. The war had been going on since 1939. Two groups of countries were fighting against each other. One group was called the Allies. The main Allies were Great Britain, France, China and the Soviet Union. The other group of countries was called the Axis. The Axis was made up of Germany, Italy and Japan. Many people wanted the United States to help the Allies, but the United States had not joined the war yet.

Johnny liked listening to the news about World War II. He thought it was exciting. The news sounded like another mystery or adventure program on the radio. The war seemed far away.

Then, on December 7, 1941, war planes from Japan attacked Pearl Harbor. Pearl Harbor is an American Navy base in Hawaii. Hawaii is a small group of islands far out in the Pacific Ocean. These islands are about halfway between Japan and the United States. Even though Hawaii is far away, it is part of the United States.

Chapter 1 The Japanese Americans: Prisoners at Home

In 1941, there were many American ships in Pearl Harbor. So when Japan attacked Pearl Harbor, it was the same as attacking the United States.

Japan bombed Pearl Harbor on December 7, 1941. It happened on a Sunday morning when most people were just waking up. The attack was a surprise. The Americans were not ready to fight back. More than 300 Japanese planes flew down out of the sky and dropped bomb after bomb on the American ships in Pearl Harbor.

The Japanese Americans
Prisoners at Home

Courtesy of NARA - Pacific Region (SF)

When the attack began, there were 94 American ships in Pearl Harbor. The ships were lined up next to each other in one part of the harbor. It was called "battleship row." The bombs exploded all around, and smoke filled the air. Sirens went off. A voice on the loudspeakers yelled, "This is an air raid! I repeat, this is an air raid! This is not a drill! Air raid!" The attack lasted for more than two hours. About 2,000 people were killed and about 1,000 people were injured. Now there were only 89 ships in the harbor. Five huge battleships were sunk.

Many of the other ships were damaged. A big part of the U.S. Navy was destroyed. It would take the United States a long time to recover from the attack.

The news of the surprise attack spread quickly. Radio stations across the United States stopped their programs to report the news. "The Japs are bombing Pearl Harbor!" shouted the radio announcers. The country was in shock.

At first, people in the United States were scared. Then they were angry at Japan. After the attack, the United States *had* to go to war. The very next day, the United States declared war on Japan. From then on, Germany, Italy, and Japan would be fighting against Great Britain, France, China, the Soviet Union, *and* the United States.

Chapter 2

Japanese Americans

Courtesy of The Bancroft Library, University of California, Berkeley

Pearl Harbor changed everything for Americans because now the United States was at war. The war was especially hard for Japanese Americans. Japanese Americans had been living in the United States for almost 60 years.

The first people from Japan to live in the United States were called *Issei*. Issei is a Japanese word that means "first generation." The *Issei* were the first generation of a family to come to the United States.

Later on, many of these Japanese Americans got married and had children in America. These children were called *Nisei. Nisei* is a Japanese word that means second generation.

Some Japanese came to the United States to go to school, but most of them came to get jobs. Most of them lived on the West Coast in California, Oregon, and Washington.

Japanese Americans worked hard. They helped to farm the land. They worked in the gold mines and silver mines.

They helped to build the railroad. They also worked in people's houses, doing jobs like cleaning and cooking and gardening. Many Japanese Americans lived in their own communities.

Johnny Ohashi was called a *Nisei* because his parents had moved to America before he was born. He was a second generation Japanese American. Johnny was 17 years old when Japan attacked Pearl Harbor. On the day of the attack, he walked into his house and found his family talking about the news.

"Johnny, did you hear the news?" his mother asked.

"What news?" asked Johnny.

"Japan attacked Pearl Harbor this morning," his mother told him.

"They say that now the United States will enter the war," added Mr. Ohashi.

"No, I don't believe it," Johnny said. "The United States would never go to war against Japan."

At that moment, a rock came crashing through the window. It landed on the floor near Johnny's feet. There was a note tied to the rock. Johnny picked up the rock and read the note.

"What does it say?" asked Mr. Ohashi.

Johnny read the note out loud. "Japs, go back to Japan!" he read. "We're not Japs," said Johnny. "We're Americans!"

Johnny's grandmother began to cry.

Chapter 2

The Japanese Americans: Prisoners at Home

The room was silent. Everybody knew that things had suddenly changed. Everything was different now. America and Japan were at war, and Japanese Americans were in big trouble.

The morning after Pearl Harbor, Johnny went to school as usual. But it was a strange day. Nobody knew what to do or say. Many of the white students refused to talk to Johnny. They didn't even look at him. Before Pearl Harbor, they had all been friends.

All the students had grown up together. Now, all of a sudden, people didn't trust each other anymore.

After school, Johnny broke up a fight between two of his friends. One was Ben Sugita. Ben was a *Nisei* like Johnny. The other student was Dave Miller. Dave was a white student. Johnny, Ben and Dave were teammates on the high school basketball team. Dave and Ben were pushing each other in the hallway, and Johnny pulled them apart.

"Hey, what's going on here?" Johnny asked Ben and Dave.

"You Japs bombed Pearl Harbor," Dave yelled. "It's because of you that we're at war."

"Who are you calling a Jap?" Ben asked.

"Both of you," replied Dave. "You're both Japs."

Johnny looked at Dave. "I don't see any Japs. I only see Americans here," said Johnny.

Courtesy of The Bancroft Library, University of California, Berkeley

"No," cried Dave. *"I'm* an American. You *two* are Japs. You Japs stay away from me. I didn't bomb Pearl Harbor." Dave was upset and ran down the hall.

"Ben and I didn't bomb Pearl Harbor either," Johnny shouted at Dave. But Dave was already gone.

Johnny and Ben knew that there were many other people like Dave who were angry and confused. These people were all scared. They didn't know who to blame for the war, so they blamed Japanese Americans.

They didn't care that Johnny and Ben were born in America. They didn't care that Johnny and Ben were American citizens.

After the fight with Dave, both Johnny and Ben decided to quit the basketball team. They didn't want any more trouble.

Chapter 3

Spying for Japan

Johnny walked home from school with his girlfriend, Sally Levine. Johnny and Sally had been going steady for six months. They planned to go to college together after high school. Even before Pearl Harbor, it was hard for them to be together because Johnny was Japanese American and Sally was white.

At that time in the United States, many people did not like to see a boy of one race dating a girl of another race. That was called an inter-racial relationship.

In most states, it was against the law for people of different races to get married.

Sally was one of the few white students who would talk to Johnny that day. They walked down the street together. It was a quiet afternoon in December, and the air felt cold. It would soon be Christmas. Johnny was happy to be with Sally. He wanted to be with her forever.

They stopped at Sally's house. Sally kissed Johnny and held him for a long time. "Don't worry," she said. "Everything will be okay."

Johnny watched Sally go into her house. Then, slowly, he walked home. He thought about what had been going on around him. Johnny *wanted* to believe that everything would be okay, but he knew that more trouble was coming.

When Johnny got home, his mother and grandmother were both crying.

"Mama!" said Johnny. "What's wrong? Where's Papa?" he asked.

"Two men from the government came and took your father away," explained Johnny's mother. "They were from the FBI." FBI stands for Federal Bureau of Investigation.

The government wanted to talk to every Japanese American who was a leader in the community. The government wanted to make sure that these Japanese Americans were not spying for Japan.

Johnny's father worked for a Japanese American newspaper, so the government thought that he might be dangerous. The government did not want Johnny's father to say anything against the war or against the United States in the newspaper.

Johnny was angry. "Where did they take him?" he asked.

"We don't know," said his grandmother. "They just took him away."

Courtesy of The Bancroft Library, University of California, Berkeley

After five days, the family got a telegram. It said that Johnny's father was in prison with many other Japanese American men. The prison was in the state of Montana. Montana is in the Rocky Mountains. Johnny's family knew that Montana was a long way from California.

The government wanted to move Japanese Americans far away from the West Coast because the West Coast of the United States is closest to Japan.

The government believed that Japanese Americans might want Japan to win the war, so they might be spies for Japan.

White people were telling stories about Japanese Americans. Nobody knew if these stories were true — the stories were only rumors. One rumor was that Japanese American fishermen were putting special bombs called *mines* in the ocean to blow up American ships. Another rumor was that Japanese Americans were sending secret radio signals.

The rumors were not true, but many people believed them anyway. These people blamed the Japanese Americans for the war. Some of these people began to attack Japanese Americans. Several Japanese Americans were beaten up in street fights. One Japanese American man was shot to death. Johnny and his family were afraid.

Chapter 4

Leaving Everything Behind

Courtesy of The Bancroft Library, University of California, Berkeley

In February 1942, President Franklin Roosevelt gave an important order. President Roosevelt's order was called Executive Order 9066. This order gave the United States Army the power to move every Japanese American citizen away from the West Coast.

Things happened quickly. Johnny's family had only ten days to get ready to move. They could not take much with them. They had to sell a lot of things in a hurry. They sold their car. They sold their beds. They sold their dishes.

They sold their tables and chairs. They sold almost everything that they owned.

People took advantage of Japanese American families during this time. People did not give them much money for their things. But since the Japanese American families had only ten days to sell their things, they sold everything fast and cheap.

Soon the day came when all of the Japanese American families had to leave San Francisco. They went to the train station early in the morning.

Chapter 4 The Japanese Americans: Prisoners at Home

Courtesy of The Bancroft Library, University of California, Berkeley

The station was very crowded, and there was a lot of confusion. The army soldiers put the families into one long line. The train slowly filled up with people.

Johnny stood on the platform at the station and took a long look around. He would not get a chance to graduate from his high school in June. He would not get a chance to go to college with Sally. He would not get a chance to be with his other friends. He would not get a chance to do a lot of things.

Chapter 4 The Japanese Americans: Prisoners at Home

Courtesy of The Bancroft Library, University of California, Berkeley

He was leaving behind everything that he knew. Sally ran up to him and grabbed his hands. They looked at each other for a long time without speaking.

"I love you, Johnny," she said.

"I love you, too," he told her.

Johnny got on the train. The train began to move, and Johnny watched Sally waving good-bye. He wondered if he would ever see her again.

The train took the Japanese American families to an old racetrack called Tanforan. The track had been used for horse races. Tanforan was about 20 miles south of San Francisco.

When they got to the racetrack, the soldiers told everyone to get off the train and to line up by the gate. Then the soldiers checked everybody's bags as they went through the gate. The ground was muddy, and people's shoes and clothes got dirty as they walked along.

Courtesy of The Bancroft Library, University of California, Berkeley

First, the families had to fill out many forms. Then each family was given a number. Johnny's family was number 13109.

A soldier told Johnny's mother to take her family to a room at the end of the racetrack. When they got to their room, they saw that it was just a stall for horses. The soldiers had quickly built walls between the stalls, and they had put boards over the dirt to make wooden floors.

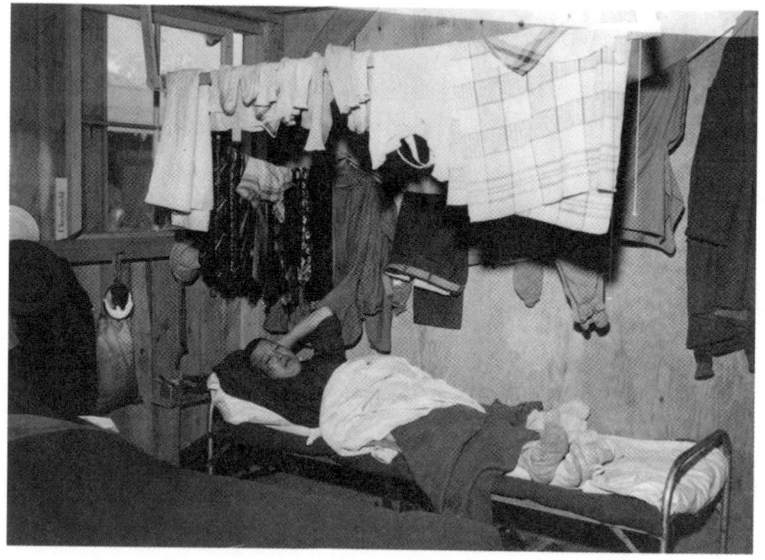

Courtesy of The Bancroft Library, University of California, Berkeley

Each stall was narrow and dark with one bare light bulb inside. Johnny's family had four small cots to sleep on.

The smell of horse manure came up through the wooden floor.

The smell made Johnny's mother feel sick. She went outside and threw up.

Chapter 5

The Racetrack

Nobody could believe that the United States government had sent Japanese Americans to live at a racetrack. This was a place for horses, not for people.

"They're treating us like animals," Johnny said. He felt so angry that he hit the wall with his fist. To his surprise, his fist went right through the wall and made a large hole! In the stall, on the other side, was Ben Sugita and his family.

"Hey, Johnny! It's so nice of you to drop in," joked Ben.

Johnny did not smile at Ben's joke. "How do they expect us to live like this?" asked Johnny.

"They say it's just for a short time," Ben answered. "They're building a prison camp for us out in the desert. We'll be moving again in a few months."

Everything at the racetrack was very crowded. People stood in long lines, and there was never enough of anything to go around. People stood in line to use the bathroom. The toilet stalls didn't have doors.

People stood in line to buy supplies, but the store always ran out of things to sell. People stood in line to wash their clothes, but there was never enough water for everyone. When there was water, everyone rushed to take showers and do their laundry. Sometimes the water was hot, but most of the time the water was cold.

Everyone ate together. People stood in line to get their food. They ate the same things every day. For breakfast, it was always oatmeal.

Courtesy of The Bancroft Library, University of California, Berkeley

One day, Johnny made a joke to the cook. “Hey,” said Johnny. “I’ve never seen oatmeal before where the spoon stood up by itself in the bowl,” he said. “Look, I think my spoon is trying to walk out of the bowl!” The food was bad, and a lot of people got sick.

After a few days, people got used to the standing and waiting. They even got used to living in stalls at the racetrack.

One afternoon, Johnny saw some young children playing. They were pretending to have a tea party. But instead of sitting around a table like other children, they were standing in line to get their tea. It made Johnny feel sad to see how quickly the children got used to things. It all seemed normal to them. Johnny wanted those children to have the chance to grow up in real homes.

Sometimes people got packages from their friends back home. The packages had food and extra clothes in them.

Johnny's family got many packages from their white neighbors in San Francisco. It made them feel good to know that people on the outside were still thinking about them.

After two months at Tanforan, the Japanese American families found out that they would soon be leaving California. The day before they left, Johnny's family heard a sudden knock on the door.

When they opened the door, they saw Johnny's father standing there. He had come back from Montana! How happy they all were to see him again!

"I'm glad that we are together," said Johnny's grandmother. "But you look so tired and thin. How long must we stay here? Our home is in San Francisco, not in this horse stall."

Chapter 6

1,000 Miles from Home

Courtesy of The Bancroft Library, University of California, Berkeley

The train ride to the desert was long. The soldiers did not want the Japanese Americans to see where they were going. When the train got near a town, the soldiers would pull down all of the shades on the windows. The train was hot and crowded inside. The trip was hard for everybody. The children cried, and the adults were tired and grumpy.

After three days, the families arrived at their new home. When they stepped off the train, they found themselves in the middle of a desert.

The bright sun hurt their eyes. The families were now in a place called Topaz, Utah. They had come more than 1,000 miles from San Francisco!

Johnny rubbed his eyes. In front of him was the prison camp. It was surrounded by a high fence that was made out of sharp barbed wire. There were guard towers every 500 feet along the fence. Inside the guard towers, Johnny could see soldiers with rifles.

The families were taken inside the prison camp. Johnny's grandmother spoke to one of the soldiers at the gate. She pointed her finger at the soldier and said, "How can you do this to us? How would you like it if you went to Tokyo in Japan, and you were treated like this?"

The soldier was much taller than Johnny's grandmother. He looked down at her and said, "This ain't Tokyo, lady."

Chapter 6 The Japanese Americans: Prisoners at Home

Courtesy of The Bancroft Library, University of California, Berkeley

The prison camp was called the Central Utah Relocation Center. It was one of ten prison camps in the United States. There were about 8,000 Japanese Americans on their way to the Utah camp. Some people were already there when Johnny's family arrived.

The camp was a big square that was one mile long and one mile wide. The Army had built many large buildings there called barracks. The barracks stood in long rows.

Each building was divided into six rooms and each family had only one room in the building.

Johnny stood in his family's room and looked around. The rooms were small, and the walls did not go all the way up to the ceiling, so Johnny could hear people talking in the next room. "There's no privacy in this place," he thought to himself.

Living in the desert was hard. It got very hot during the day. Then, at night, it got very cold. But the worst part was the dust storms.

Courtesy of The Bancroft Library, University of California, Berkeley

Every afternoon, the wind would begin to howl. The wind would pick up the dirt and blow it all around until everything was covered with white dust. People ran inside the barracks, but the dust came in through the cracks in the walls. Dust got into people's hair. It got underneath their clothes. Dust even got into the food.

"Living at the prison camp in the desert is even *worse* than living at the racetrack," thought Johnny. But after a few weeks, Johnny and everyone else at the camp started to get used to it.

Courtesy of The Bancroft Library, University of California, Berkeley

People began to organize themselves into groups called committees. They chose leaders to speak for them. They collected old pieces of wood to build the things that they needed. They started their own schools for both children and adults. They started teams to play basketball and other games.

Even though they were in a prison camp, the Japanese American families tried to help each other and live together in a peaceful way. They tried to make a community in the camp.

Chapter 7

Grandmother's Story

Johnny's grandmother sometimes told stories to the children at bedtime. One night, she asked the children to sit in a circle on the ground outside the barracks. "Look up at the moon and stars," she told the children. "Do you see all those stars that are next to the moon? They look like a frozen river, don't they?" she asked. "That river of stars is called the Milky Way. In Japan, we always told a story about the moon and stars at this time of year."

"Would you tell us the story?" asked one of the girls.

"Well," began Grandmother, "once upon a time, there was a beautiful princess who lived in the sky. That bright star over there is *her* star," said Grandmother, pointing at a star on one side of the Milky Way.

"The Princess liked to weave beautiful cloth for her father," continued Grandmother. "He was the Sky God. One day, the Princess saw a handsome man across the river. He was a herdsman and he was taking care of a large herd of cattle on the other side of the river. The Princess fell in love with the herdsman."

"I see *his* star!" said one of the children pointing to the brightest star on the other side of the Milky Way.

Grandmother went on with her story. "The Sky God brought the herdsman across the Milky Way to marry his daughter. But, after the wedding, the daughter was so happy with her new husband that she stopped weaving cloth for her father. Her father became so angry that he sent the herdsman back to the other side of the river," said Grandmother.

"Then what happened?" asked another child.

"The Princess begged the Sky God to let her live with her husband," said Grandmother. "Finally, the Sky God agreed to do this. He said that he would send a boat to bring the herdsman back, but just for one day each year. The moon is the boat that will take him across the river. That is why the moon is so close to the Milky Way at this time of year," she explained.

One of the older boys spoke up. “The herdsman only got to see his wife once a year,” he said. “I want to go home and be with my friends all the time.”

“You will be free someday, my children,” said Grandmother. “But things will be different. You might never see your old friends again.”

Chapter 8

Death Comes to the Desert

During the summer, people in the prison camp tried to plant flowers and trees, but their flowers and trees would not grow in the desert. The wind blew all the young plants away. The soil was too dry to keep them green, and all of the plants died quickly.

By October, it began to get cold. The sun stayed lower in the sky and the days became shorter. There was snow on the mountain tops in the distance.

Soon it became too cold and windy to keep the schools open, so the children didn't have anything to do. Most of the adults just sat in their rooms all day. They had no hope. Some of them cried. One old man was so sad that he took a rope and tried to hang himself in his room.

Since the children could not go to school, they spent their time playing. Children stopped doing things with their parents. During the meals in the big dining hall, the children all sat together.

They didn't want to sit with their parents anymore. Families began to fall apart.

There was not enough coal to keep the camp warm or to make enough hot water. The people had hot water for only two hours in the morning. During those two hours, everyone ran to take showers. Some people didn't share things with others. They stopped helping each other, and started keeping extra things just for themselves. Other people didn't trust their neighbors anymore.

Courtesy of The Bancroft Library, University of California, Berkeley

Fights started. People were afraid of being robbed. The community began to fall apart.

The week before Christmas, Johnny received a package from Sally. Johnny was very happy to hear from her. She sent him a sweater and some cookies. At the bottom of the package was a long letter. She told him that things were very bad at home in San Francisco. There was not enough food there either. Each family was only allowed to buy a small amount of food and supplies.

People on the West Coast were afraid of a Japanese attack. "We have air raid drills," wrote Sally. "That means that we pretend that we are being attacked. At night, we have to turn off all the lights. If everything is dark, the enemy pilots from Japan can't see where they're going," Sally wrote.

Sally also wrote that Dave Miller was dead. After Pearl Harbor, Dave had joined the Army.

"Dave was a good soldier," Sally continued. "He was killed when he jumped out of an airplane and his parachute didn't open."

The news about Dave made Johnny sad. He remembered their fight in the school hallway, but most of all, Johnny remembered Dave as a friend. They had grown up together. Johnny wished that things could have ended better between them.

That winter was hard for everybody. But it was hardest for the old people. Many of them got sick.

Johnny's grandmother caught a bad cold. Her lungs became infected, and her chest hurt when she tried to breathe. Soon she was so sick that she died.

The funeral was short. Some of the other women decorated the coffin with paper flowers. Grandmother was buried outside the barbed wire fence in the desert. Johnny's family was only allowed to spend 15 minutes at her grave.

Johnny and his parents kneeled down next to Grandmother's grave. Johnny looked back at the prison camp. He could see all of their footprints in the snow leading to the grave. He closed his eyes and felt the sharp cold wind blowing against his face. He remembered his grandmother's words: "You will be free someday, but things will be different."

Johnny wanted to leave the prison camp more than anything else in the world. He felt like running away into the mountains.

Chapter 9

No-no Boys

Soon after the new year, Johnny got his chance to leave the prison camp. At the beginning of the war, the government had said that Japanese Americans couldn't join the Army. But in February 1943, the government changed its rule and said that Japanese Americans *could* be soldiers. They would be in a special group. This group was called the all-Nisei 442nd Regiment. The Army was now looking for volunteers. They were looking for men who wanted to join the 442nd.

Johnny volunteered to join. He wanted to leave the prison camp. He wanted to prove that he was an American. He wanted to prove that he was loyal to America. Johnny's parents were worried about him, but they decided to let him join the Army.

About 1,200 Japanese American men volunteered from all of the camps. Many of them were from Johnny's camp. A week later, Johnny said good-bye to his family and left on a bus with the other volunteers from Topaz, Utah.

Courtesy of The Bancroft Library, University of California, Berkeley

A month later, the government began to *force* young men in the prison camps to join the Army. Everybody had to answer a list of questions. But many Japanese American men had problems with question 27 and question 28.

Question 27 asked if they would be willing to fight whenever they were sent into battle. Question 28 asked if they could promise that they would not be on Japan's side in the war.

This question asked Japanese American men to promise that they would be loyal to the United States and not to Japan.

Ben Sugita did not volunteer for the Army. He refused to let the Army make him fight. He answered "no" to both questions. People who did this were called "no-no boys." They were arrested and put in an army prison. That is what happened to Ben.

At his trial, Ben spoke to the judge. Ben said, "My family and I are American citizens. All American citizens have the right to be free. But you have taken away our rights. The government has put my family in a prison camp, and now you want to force me to fight for America," explained Ben. "I will not fight for America until my family is free. I would rather go to prison!"

So Ben was sent to prison with the other "no-no boys."

While Ben was in prison, Johnny was in basic training in the Army. One day, he wrote this letter to his parents:

Dear Mom and Dad,

I am fine. I am writing from the state of Mississippi. We are done with basic training here. We are now on our way to Italy to fight in the war. We are all Nisei here in the 442nd. There are about 6,000 of us in my division. We are all excited and a little scared.

But please don't worry about me. Everything will be fine. I will see you again when the war is over.

Love,

Johnny

The 442nd became one of the most famous regiments in the American Army. Many Japanese Americans joined it. The motto of the 442nd was "Go for broke." They helped fight in many battles. Almost 9,500 Japanese Americans were killed in the war.

Japanese American soldiers earned many medals. One of the medals was called the Congressional Medal of Honor. This medal was given to Sadao Munemori. He died while saving other soldiers from a hand grenade that had landed near him. Only 29 soldiers got the Congressional Medal of Honor during World War II.

In 1944, the 442nd Regiment helped to free 300 American soldiers who were trapped in the mountains in France. The trapped men were called the "Lost Battalion."

The men had been surrounded by the German army for many weeks. The 442nd saved the Lost Battalion. But many, many Japanese American soldiers were killed in the battle, and many other Nisei soldiers were missing after the battle. Johnny was one of these missing soldiers.

Johnny's parents got a telegram from the United States Army. The telegram said that Johnny Ohashi was missing in action.

Chapter 10

After the War

On August 6, 1945, the United States dropped an atomic bomb on the city of Hiroshima, Japan. Three days later, the United States dropped a second atomic bomb on Nagasaki, Japan. The two atomic bombs killed or injured nearly 200,000 Japanese people and destroyed both cities. Japan was defeated. On August 15, Japan surrendered to the United States. World War II was over.

In late October 1945, the Japanese American families were released from Topaz, Utah.

As Johnny's parents walked toward the gate on that day, they saw Johnny standing there! They couldn't believe it! They ran up to greet him. Johnny and his family hugged each other as people walked past them.

Johnny had been a part of the battle to free the Lost Battalion. He had been injured when a hand grenade exploded near him. After the battle, he had been rescued and sent to a hospital. His arm was hurt so badly that the doctors had to cut it off.

The left sleeve of Johnny's Army uniform was pinned across the front of his shirt. The words "United States of America" were written on the sleeve, so it looked like Johnny was wearing a banner across his chest.

"I told you that I would see you again after the war," Johnny said to his parents.

Johnny walked out of the prison camp with his parents. The two soldiers at the gate saluted Johnny as he walked past.

Courtesy of The Bancroft Library, University of California, Berkeley

After the war, Johnny Ohashi and his parents moved back to San Francisco. They had spent more than three years away. They had to start all over again. Things would never be the same as before the war. But they did everything they could to make a good life together.

Johnny went to college to study law, and he became a lawyer. He became a leader in the fight for justice for Japanese Americans.

Japanese Americans wanted the United States government to apologize for putting them into prison camps during World War II.

Japanese American families lost many things when they were sent to the camps. They lost their homes. They lost members of their families. They lost three years of their lives. And many Japanese Americans lost their trust in the government. Johnny and the other leaders argued that the government of the United States owed Japanese Americans an apology.

In court, Johnny said, "Ten people from the United States were spies for Japan during World War II. All ten of them were white. Not one of them was Japanese American. What you did to us was wrong!"

More than 40 years after World War II, the government passed a law called the Civil Rights act of 1988. The government said that it was sorry for the way that Japanese Americans had been treated.

The government also gave $20,000 to each person from the prison camps who was still alive. The money did not come close to what the Japanese American families had lost. But they still felt that they had won something important.

After college, Johnny and Sally got married. A few years later, they had a daughter named Monica. When Monica was five years old, Johnny took her back to Utah to visit the old Topaz prison camp.

Courtesy of The Bancroft Library, University of California, Berkeley

The barbed wire fence was gone. Most of the barracks had been torn down. Johnny and Monica found some broken dishes in the dirt where the dining hall had been.

"You lived here?" Monica asked her father.

"Yes," answered Johnny. "And your grandpa and grandma lived here for over three years," he said.

"It must have been lonely," said Monica. "What was it like?" she asked.

"Close your eyes," her father answered. "Do you hear the wind howling? That was the sound that we heard day and night," he said.

Johnny held Monica's hand as they walked to Grandmother's grave. They put a flower on the grave.

"Your great-grandmother is buried here," he said.

"Do you remember her?" Monica asked.

"Yes, I remember her very well," Johnny answered. "And she would want me to tell you this, Monica. You must always make the most of your freedom. You can do anything that you want in your life. Don't be afraid."

The End

A Note from the Start-to-Finish Editors

You will notice that Start-to-Finish Books look different from other high-low readers and chapter books. The text layout of this book coordinates with the other media components (CD and audiocassette) of the Start-to-Finish series.

The text in the book matches, line-for-line and page-for-page, the text shown on the computer screen, enabling readers to follow along easily in the book. Each page ends in a complete sentence so that the student can either practice the page (repeat reading) or turn the page to continue with the story. If the next sentence cannot fit on the page in its entirety, it has been shifted to the next page. For this reason, the sentence at the top of a page may not be indented, signaling that it is part of the paragraph from the preceding page.

Words are not hyphenated at the ends of lines. This sometimes creates extra space at the end of a line, but eliminates confusion for the struggling reader.